Mice on Ice

I LIKE TO READ is a registered trademark of Holiday House, Inc.
Copyright © 2012 by Rebecca Emberley and Ed Emberley
All Rights Reserved
HOLIDAY HOUSE is registered in the U.S. Patent and Trademark Office.
Printed and Bound in April 2013 at Tien Wah Press, Johor Bahru, Johor, Malaysia.
The text typeface is Shannon.
The artwork was created digitally and with cut paper.
www.holidayhouse.com
3 5 7 9 10 8 6 4 2

Library of Congress Cataloging-in-Publication Data
Emberley, Rebecca.
Mice on ice / by Rebecca Emberley and Ed Emberley. — 1st ed.
p. cm. — (I like to read)
Summary: Colorful mice go ice skating and are unexpectedly joined by a feline
friend.
ISBN 978-0-8234-2576-1 (hardcover)
[1. Stories in rhyme. 2. Ice skating—Fiction. 3. Mice—Fiction. 4. Cats—Fiction.]
I. Emberley, Ed. II. Title.
PZ8.3.E517Mi 2012
782.42—dc23
[E]
2011038812

ISBN 978-0-8234-2908-0 (paperback)
GRL C

Mice
on
Ice

by Rebecca Emberley and Ed Emberley

I Like to Read®

Holiday House / New York

Mice walk on snow.

Mice skate on ice.

Mice on ice look nice.

Mice are skating.

Someone is waiting.

What is this?

What is that?

That is a cat.

That is a cat with a hat.

The cat with a hat skates
with mice on ice.

Nice!

I Like to Read® Books
You will like all of them!

Boy, Bird, and Dog by David McPhail

Dinosaurs Don't, Dinosaurs Do
        by Steve Björkman

Fish Had a Wish by Michael Garland

The Fly Flew In by David Catrow

I Will Try by Marilyn Janovitz

Late Nate in a Race by Emily Arnold McCully

The Lion and the Mice
        by Rebecca Emberley and Ed Emberley

Mice on Ice
        by Rebecca Emberley and Ed Emberley

Pig Has a Plan by Ethan Long

See Me Run by Paul Meisel

Sick Day by David McPhail

Visit holidayhouse.com to learn more
about I Like to Read® Books.

I Like to Read® Books in Paperback
You will like all of them!

Boy, Bird, and Dog by David McPhail
Dinosaurs Don't, Dinosaurs Do
      by Steve Björkman
Fish Had a Wish by Michael Garland
The Fly Flew In by David Catrow
I Will Try by Marilyn Janovitz
Late Nate in a Race
      by Emily Arnold McCully
The Lion and the Mice by Rebecca Emberley
      and Ed Emberley
Mice on Ice by Rebecca Emberley
      and Ed Emberley
Pig Has a Plan by Ethan Long
See Me Run by Paul Meisel
      a Theodor Seuss Geisel Award Honor Book
Sick Day by David McPhail

Visit holidayhouse.com to learn more
about I Like to Read® Books.